Wagons Ho!
A Diary of the Oregon Trail

Cynthia Mercati

Perfection Learning®

Cover and Inside Illustrations: Larassa Kabel

About the Author

Cynthia Mercati is a writer and a professional actress. She has written many plays for a children's theatre that tours and performs at various schools. She also appears in many of the plays herself.

Ms. Mercati loves reading about history and visiting historical places. When she writes a historical play or book, she wants her readers to feel like they are actually living the story.

Ms. Mercati also loves baseball. Her favorite team is the Chicago White Sox. She grew up in Chicago, Illinois, but she now lives in Des Moines, Iowa. Ms. Mercati has two children and one dog.

Contents

March 1, 1849 4

March 10, 1849 7

April 11, 1849 12

April 27, 1849 14

May 10, 1849 19

June 23, 1849 23

July 4, 1849 26

July 18, 1849 28

July 30, 1849 31

August 3, 1849 35

Sometime in September 1849 39

Sometime in September 1849 40

Sometime in Late September 1849 44

Sometime in Early October 1849 46

October 18, 1849 48

The Oregon Trail 51

Glossary 53

March 1, 1849

It's my tenth birthday today! This diary was my present from Ma and Pa. The pen I'm writing with was a present from my older brother. His name is Seth.

I have a sister too. Her name is Opal. She's only five. My name is Liza.

I will have many exciting things to write. In just nine days, we're leaving. Our family is going to start out for the Oregon Territory! We live in Illinois now.

I've never been farther away than ten miles from our farm. Now I'm going to travel clear across the country!

4

Pa read all about Oregon in the newspaper. Then he told us about it.

"The forests in Oregon are thick with tall timber," Pa said. "I could build us a fine cabin. The soil is rich and black. All the land is free for the takin'. We could have a big farm there!"

"What's the weather like?" Ma asked.

"The summers aren't nearly as hot they are here," Pa answered. "The winters aren't as cold."

"That sounds good to me," Ma said.

Pa grinned at us. "People say the potatoes grow as big as pumpkins in Oregon! They say the livin' is so easy there. In fact, pigs run around already cooked!"

Everyone laughed.

"Oregon must be paradise on earth," Seth said.

"It sure must be," Ma agreed. "I reckon we better go there!"

Pa nodded. "I reckon we better!"

That night, I was so excited. I could hardly get to sleep. I couldn't wait to see paradise for myself!

March 10, 1849

Pa sold our farm to buy a wagon. This is how we'll get to Oregon!

The wagon is called a **Conestoga**. It has high wooden boards on each side. Its wheels are rimmed with iron and painted red. They're as tall as Opal!

A thick white canvas cover tops our wagon. The cover stretches tightly between six wooden hoops. Ma and I sewed it ourselves!

I think our wagon looks like a boat. Opal thinks it looks like a loaf of bread!

Pa also bought six oxen to pull our wagon. They're **yoked** together in teams of two.

"Oxen don't go very fast," Pa said. "But they're strong! They'll be able to stand the trip much better than horses could."

Inside our wagon, we packed big sacks of flour and beans, a wooden washtub, and a big iron kettle. We also packed our sleeping **pallets** and quilts.

Ma, Opal, and I will sleep inside the wagon. Seth and Pa will sleep under it.

Our **grub** box is right up front. We can get to it quickly! Inside we packed slabs of bacon and jars of dried fruit and jelly. We also put in tin buckets filled with brown sugar, **lard**, coffee, and salt.

Ma's pots and pans hang on hooks on the outside of the wagon. Our water keg hangs there too.

Pa tied a big wooden box beneath the wagon. Inside are his tools and some spare wagon parts.

Ma cried when she found out there was no room for her china cabinet. And she couldn't take her rocking chair either.

My grandparents came to say good-bye the morning we left. All our neighbors came too.

Ma climbed up on the wagon seat. She took the reins in her hand. Opal climbed in next to her.

Seth tied up our two milk cows to the back of the wagon. He'll walk behind the wagon to guide the animals along. Pa will walk up front, next to the oxen.

I got into the back of the wagon. Daisy, our dog, jumped in beside me.

"Go safely," Grandmother said. "Once you're settled in Oregon, your grandfather and I are going to come out. We'll all live together on your big, new farm!"

Everyone was waving good-bye. I got a lump in my throat. It was hard to say good-bye to my friends.

For the first time, I felt scared and sad. We were leaving behind everyone and everything we knew.

And who knew what was waiting for us on the trail.

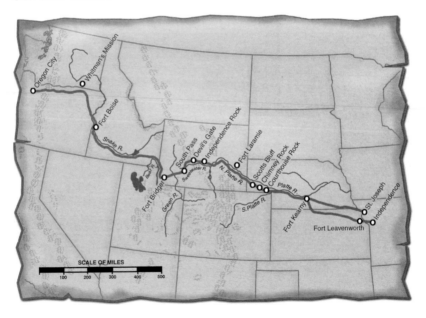

April 11, 1849

We have finally reached Independence, Missouri!

It's too dangerous for just one wagon to travel west alone. So people meet in Independence. There they form big **caravans** of wagons. These caravans are called *wagon trains*.

We have joined one of the trains. There will be 50 wagons in ours!

A man has been hired to head our wagon train. He's led people to Oregon several times before. His name is Tom McCullough. We all call him Captain McCullough.

The morning we left Independence, Captain McCullough got us up before sunrise! He sounded a blast on his trumpet.

Ma cooked us breakfast. Opal and I rolled up our bedding. Seth and Pa watered and fed the oxen. Then they hitched them to the wagon.

I picked up Daisy. Opal and I scrambled onto the seat next to Ma.

"Wagons ho!" Captain McCullough shouted. A cheer went up.

Pa called out to the lead oxen. "Gee, Bet! Gee, Blue!" He cracked his whip over the oxen's backs. They lurched forward. The wheels started turning. The pots and pans started clattering! We were on our way!

Pa smiled back at us. "Oregon or bust!" he shouted.

April 27, 1849

We're crossing the **Great Plains** now!

The sky is low and big. I feel like I could reach right up and grab a cloud!

All around us is tall prairie grass. It shines green-gold in the sun. It ripples like the waves of the ocean in the wind. Through this sea of grass, our wagons roll along like ships at sea.

Riding in the wagon is so bumpy. It makes my teeth rattle! Opal and I walk most of the time. Daisy runs next to us. There are lots of other children to talk to and play with.

All the spare oxen, saddle horses, and cows are at the back of the line. They call the *cow column*. Seth and the older boys have to herd the cow column along.

Fifty wagons can really kick up dust! Captain McCullough has made a rule. First in line goes to the end of the line the next day. Then each day, you move up a place until you're in front again.

When the sun climbs high in the sky, we stop for lunch. We eat a cold meal of biscuits and jam. And we rest in the shade.

When we make camp for the night, we turn the wagons into a circle. On a good day, we make 12 miles!

There are hardly any trees on the plains. We have to use cow chips for our cooking fires! (That's a nice word for dried cow dung!) It's Opal's job to collect the cow chips in a big basket.

We always try to make camp by a river or stream. Opal and I have to fetch the water. Seth has to help Pa take care of the oxen.

Each night, I take down the bucket of axle grease from underneath the wagon seat. Then I grease each wagon wheel. I also have to check each spoke for cracks.

After supper, all the children run from wagon to wagon. Seth visits with his friends. The women talk a blue streak while mending. The men smoke their pipes and swap stories.

On Sundays, we rest. Captain McCullough reads a chapter from the Bible to all of us.

Ma bakes up a pie. That's her day to bake bread too.

It's also washing day for clothes and people! A line is strung between our wagon and the wagon next to us. That's where we hang the wash.

Then Ma heats up more water in the kettle. She pours it into the big tub. One by one, we climb in for our weekly baths. It sure feels good to get the dust off!

Some of the men have brought along their fiddles and banjos. I love it when they start playing around the campfire! Everyone claps and sings. Some people dance.

Pa and Ma even did a do-si-do! I usually grab Opal or one of my friends. We whirl around until we're dizzy and laughing! Daisy barks and jumps.

Sometimes to put myself to sleep, I quietly hum one of the fiddle tunes.

Buffalo gals, won't you come out tonight?
Come out tonight? Come out tonight?
Buffalo gals, won't you come out tonight?
And dance by the light of the moon!

May 10, 1849

Earlier, we were taking our noon rest. Suddenly, I heard thunder. But the sky was clear!

Captain McCullough came riding down the line.

"Swing the wagons in a circle!" he called out. "It's a buffalo stampede!"

A big, whirling cloud of dust was headed our way. Inside the dust cloud were the buffalo!

In what seemed like a few seconds, the wagons were in a circle. Ma grabbed Opal. I grabbed Daisy. Pa and Seth grabbed their guns from under the wagon seat. We all ducked under the wagon. Pa and Seth lay flat behind the wheels.

"We have to turn them!" Captain McCullough shouted.

The swirling dust drew ever nearer. Now I could see the great animals up close.

They were packed tight. Their shaggy heads were down. Their tails were in the air. The ground trembled under their hooves.

"Fire!" Captain McCullough shouted. The crack of rifles sliced the air.

The line of buffalo in the front of the pack fell to the ground. Then more went down. But more kept coming! It looked like they were going to plow right into our wagons!

"Fire!" Captain McCullough yelled. Again rifle shouts barked in the air.

I squeezed Dasiy so close she yelped. Opal was crying. Ma hugged her tight. Then she hugged me.

At Captain McCullough's order, the men fired again.

The gunshots were working. The line of shaggy animals split in the middle. They raced away from the pile of dead buffalo and past the wagons. Dust blew into our mouths and down our throats.

Finally, the last of the herd galloped by. The dust settled. The pounding of hundreds of hooves faded out.

Slowly, people crawled out from under their wagons.

Seth gave a long, low whistle. "That was a close call!"

June 23, 1849

We have passed Courthouse Rock and Chimney Rock. They're piles of red sandstone. We're in Wyoming Territory now!

We've also had our first bad storm. The sky turned black as midnight. Sheets of lightning lit up the land like fireworks!

The women crawled inside the wagons. The men stayed with the oxen. The rain seeped through our canvas cover. The wind blew so hard, it shook the wagon.

After the rain, the trail was a muddy mess! The wet brought the mosquitoes out something fierce. They swarmed over the oxen's heads and drove us crazy!

A few days later, we rolled into Fort Laramie. We're now 700 miles from Independence!

Fort Laramie is made of **adobe**. There's a big gate at the entrance. The walls are slit with loopholes for rifles to poke through.

Inside the fort, Ma bought flour and sugar at the **sutler's** shop. Pa had some tools repaired at the blacksmith's shop.

We saw many Sioux Indians at the fort. Some were there to trade. Lots of the men worked as horse **wranglers**.

Captain McCullough says Fort Laramie is the last outpost of civilization until we reach Oregon. His words make me shiver. There's no turning back now!

July 4, 1849

We timed it just right. We're camped near Independence Rock on our nation's birthday!

After we left Fort Laramie, the road was stony and steep. For a week, we traveled upward.

Then we saw Independence Rock! It was standing boldly against the sky!

The rock was named by an early party of traders who camped here on July 4. Captain McCullough scratched the name of our wagon train and the date into the famous rock.

We're in the mountains now! Tall cliffs rise up on either side of us. Many of the earlier wagon trains had to lighten their loads to make it up the trail. Scattered pieces of furniture are everywhere. We also see ovens, mirrors, plows, clothes, books. There was even a piano!

We are seeing more and more graves. One grave was marked with a wagon seat. On it were written the words "Oregon or Death." We passed that grave in silence.

July 18, 1849

Today as we creaked along, Captain McCullough fired a rifle shot. That's the signal for the train to stop.

Sitting tall in the saddle, Captain McCullough pointed to the valley ahead. Between the bare hills ran a stream.

"That's the **Continental Divide**," the captain called out.

"What does that mean?" Opal asked. Her eyes were wide.

"It means we're really, truly in the West," Pa answered. He sounded excited. "From here on in, all the rivers and streams will flow westward toward the Pacific Ocean!"

"Maybe that will help pull us along to Oregon!" Opal said.

The next day we came to a long, steep hill. We stopped at the very top. The women and children scrambled down on our knees and our bottoms! The men lowered the wagons down on ropes, one at a time.

Pa and Seth locked the wheels of our wagon with poles. But still it slid like a sled! The oxen had to run at a swift clip to keep in front!

Several of the wagons overturned. One was so wrecked it had to be turned into a two-wheel cart.

I don't know which is worse. Going down the mountains or climbing up!

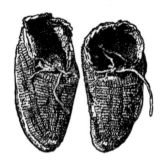

July 30, 1849

A party of Indian men visited our camp last night!

At the sight of them, the fiddles came to a stop. So did the banjos. So did all the people. We just stood and stared.

Their chests were bare. Their black hair was braided. They wore deerskin **leggings** and **moccasins**.

"They're not wearing war paint," Seth whispered to me.

"They're Crow," Captain McCullough explained. "I know some of their **lingo**. I know some sign language too. I'll see what they want."

The captain found out they wanted to trade their fresh buffalo meat for our supplies.

Lots of people on the train wanted to trade! Pa gave them some of our sugar for their meat.

Was I glad! We haven't had any fresh game since the buffalo stampede. I was getting mighty tired of eating beans and bacon every day. What I wouldn't give for a piece of fresh fruit!

Ma also traded some of our coffee for a pair of moccasins for me! My shoes are worn to a frazzle. My new moccasins are covered with beautiful beads. They're as comfortable as butter!

One of the Indians pointed to a corset hanging on a clothesline. He asked Captain McCullough what it was. The captain explained it was a lady's underwear. All the Crow had a good laugh. So did we!

Before the Indians left, they gave Captain McCullough a buffalo robe as a gift.

Seth, Opal, and I watched the Indians ride off.

"I sure do admire the way they sit on their horses," Seth said. I did too.

I wiggled my toes in my new moccasins. I was glad I'd have something to remember our visitors by.

August 3, 1849

We're in Idaho Territory. All I can see is yellow sand and gray sagebrush.

We have to use the sagebrush to start our cooking fires. It smells ten times worse than cow chips!

The sun is like blazing brass. Heat waves dance in front of our eyes.

Opal and I drag through the days. We put one foot in front of the other without knowing what we're doing. Daisy plods next to us with her tongue hanging out.

The ground is rough and dry. It rubbed my ankles raw! So I've taken to wearing a pair of Seth's old trousers and one of his old shirts. Ma was a little mad, but not much.

No one cares about looking pretty anymore. We can't even stay clean! Seth brags that he hasn't combed his hair since Nebraska!

My sunbonnet is hot. It makes my head itch. But I have to wear it.

"If you don't," Ma said, "your skin will get even more sunburned and freckled! And everyone knows you can tell a real lady by the whiteness of her skin!"

I wish I didn't have to worry about being a lady until we reach Oregon!

Water is very scarce. We have to ration it. We can't find a stream or a creek to camp by. Everyone is **parched**, including the animals.

One night, Captain McCullough told us we all had to lighten our loads. "We still have two more mountain ranges to cross," he said. "The Blues and the Cascades. And the oxen are already lookin' mighty poorly."

We had a family meeting to decide what to keep and what had to go. We decided we needed our food, our tools, the wagon parts, and our sleeping gear.

"We don't need my good dishes," Ma said.
She stood up and went into the wagon. She
came out carrying her china. She threw it to
the side of the trail. Then she sat down by the
campfire and cried.

Sometime in September 1849

I have lost track of the days. So has everyone else! We have come to the Snake River. We'll follow it for the next 300 miles.

One day, the trail split off. The left fork went to California. The right fork continued on to Oregon. About ten of our wagons took the right fork.

Oregon, Oregon, Oregon. Sometimes it seems like I've been trying to get there my whole life!

Sometime in September 1849

We've gotten across Three Island Crossing!

The islands divide the river into four **channels**. Captain McCullough led the wagons into the water one at a time. Pa and Seth had to swim the oxen across.

Ma, Opal, and I rode in the wagon.

I had butterflies in my stomach when it was our turn. River crossings are always dangerous.

We made it across the first
good shape. But by the time w
second one, the water was flow
knees!

Finally, we came to the last c_____.

The **current** was swift and strong. I could
feel it turning the wagon this way and that. I
buried my face in Daisy's fur. I was sure we
were going under!

But then I felt the wagon straighten itself
out again. I squeezed Opal's hand. Everything
was going to be okay!

was then we heard the scream! The woman in the wagon behind us had fallen into the water!

Her husband jumped in after her. Captain McCullough jumped in too. After that, it was all a blur of noise and movement. The woman's screams! The men shouting to her! The sound of the river! The woman splashing and thrashing!

I saw the woman grab hold of the captain's hand! But the current was too powerful. She was washed away from the men.

The river had won.

Some of the men planted torches on the opposite bank so the last wagons could cross in the dark. It was late at night by the time everyone was across. Everyone was thinking of the woman who had drowned.

The next morning, I talked to Pa about it.

"It's so sad," I said. "Her family will have to make a home in Oregon alone."

"Lots of sad things have happened on this trail," Pa said. "Frightenin' things too."

"If you'd known how hard this trip was going to be," I asked, "would you still have wanted to come?"

Pa rubbed his whiskered chin. Finally, he nodded.

"I like to see new things, Liza," Pa said. "I reckon that's how most of us are in this country! We've always got to be goin' on to somethin' new. Lookin' for what's over the next mountain. Around the next bend in the river!"

I think about what Pa said. About how Americans like to find new places, try new things.

All in all, it sounds like a good way to be!

Sometime in Late September 1849

For two days, we climbed up the Blue Mountains. Opal was so disappointed.

They're not really blue. From a distance they have a bluish haze. But up close, they're covered with pine forests.

We came down to the green Grande Ronde Valley. It was so beautiful! I wish we could have stayed. But the next day, on we went into **plateau** country. This land is so bare. There's nothing for the oxen to graze on.

The animals are so thin. Their ribs are sticking out! People are thin too! We're not going to get any fatter either. We're almost out of food.

Some of the wagons have lost their covers. But ours is still in place. Ma and I are proud of how strong we made it!

Night after night, I dream about a real house with a real roof and real walls!

Sometime in Early October 1849

Almost there! Almost there!

The road we followed through the Cascade Mountains was a rough one! It was choked with stumps and boulders. We went up—up. Up through tall stands of pines and cedars and firs. Then down we went again. Then up again over sharp rocks and tree roots and fallen logs. Then down again.

There were several rushing, roaring streams to cross! The men had to tie ropes to the wagons and pull them across to the other side!

The nights are cold now. In the mornings, there's ice on the wagon wheels.

Sometimes we have to walk through snow. But it isn't deep. A cold wind blows all the time. Most of us have thrown our warm clothes away to lighten the wagons! By the time we make camp, we're chilled to the bone.

I pray we make it to Oregon before the first snowstorm. It could mean death for all of us if we're stranded in the mountains in a blizzard.

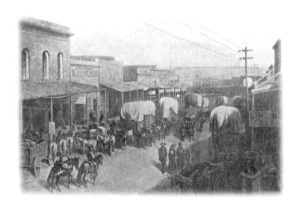

October 18, 1849

We made it! We're at the end of the trail! Today, creaking and groaning, our wagons rolled into Oregon City! People came out of their houses to say "Hello!"

Oregon truly is paradise! It's green everywhere! The air is soft. It's filled with the scent of pine trees.

Pa bought us a tent. We'll sleep in that until Pa and Seth can build us a cabin.

Before I crawled into the tent tonight, I sat outside to write these lines. Daisy was right next to me. Just like she's been every step of the way from Illinois.

I sure have learned a lot on this journey! I've seen a lot too. I reckon I couldn't have helped but grown up a lot!

I looked up at the sky. The Oregon sky! Then I gave Daisy a pat.

"We're home," I whispered.

THE OREGON TRAIL

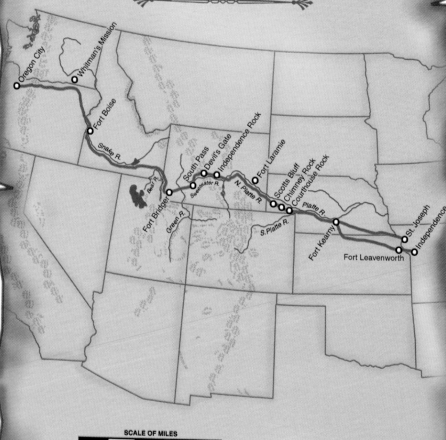

Oregon City

Whitman's Mission

Fort Boise

Snake R.

South Pass

Devil's Gate

Independence Rock

Fort Laramie

Scotts Bluff

Chimney Rock

Courthouse Rock

Fort Bridger

Sweetwater R.

N. Platte R.

Bear R.

Green R.

Platte R.

S. Platte R.

Fort Kearny

St. Joseph

Independence

Fort Leavenworth

SCALE OF MILES

100   200   300   400   500

The Oregon Trail

The family in this diary traveled from Illinois to Oregon. These are some of the important places along the Oregon Trail.

Independence, Missouri
Fort Kearny, Nebraska
Courthouse Rock
Chimney Rock
Scotts Bluff
Fort Laramie, Wyoming
Independence Rock
Devil's Gate
South Pass
Fort Bridger
Rocky Mountains

Continental Divide
Fort Boise
Blue Mountains
Cascade Mountains
Snake River
Grande Ronde Valley
Columbia River
Whitman's Mission
The Dalles
Willamette Valley
Oregon City

The family also went through many states and territories. Listed below are the years the territories they traveled through became states.

Missouri	1821
Kansas	1861
Nebraska	1867
Wyoming	1890
Idaho	1890
Washington	1889
Oregon	1859

Glossary

adobe   brick made of sun-dried earth and straw

caravan   group of vehicles and/or people traveling together

channel   stream of water between two close pieces of land

Conestoga   large canvas-topped wagon named after Conestoga, Pennsylvania, where the wagons were made

Continental Divide also called the backbone of a continent. In North America, the great ridge of the Rocky Mountains separates the streams and rivers flowing westward toward the Pacific Ocean from those flowing eastward toward the Atlantic.

current swiftest part of a stream or river

ford to cross water

Great Plains high grasslands. They include the western part of North Dakota, South Dakota, Nebraska, Kansas, and Oklahoma and the eastern part of Montana, Wyoming, Colorado, New Mexico, and Texas.

grub   food

lard   soft, white, solid or semi-solid
               fat. It usually comes from
               butchering a hog.

leggings   covering for the legs made of
               leather

lingo   language

moccasin   soft leather shoe

pallet   straw-filled mattress

parched   dried up; thirsty

plateau   high area of land with a flat
               surface

sutler   shopkeeper on an army post

wrangler   someone who takes care of
               horses

yoke to hold together by a wooden bar. Usually two animals are held together at the neck so they can work as a team.